P9-DVG-308

Lucy & Tom's Christmas

SHIRLEY HUGHES

VIKING KESTREL

In loving memory of Sally

VIKING KESTREL

Viking Penguin Inc., 40 West 23rd Street, New York, New York 10010, U.S.A.

First published in Great Britain by Victor Gollancz Ltd 1981
First American Edition
Published in 1986
Copyright © Shirley Hughes, 1981
All rights reserved
Printed in Hong Kong by South China Printing Co.

Library of Congress catalog card number: 86-40023
(CIP data available)
ISBN 0-670-81255-2

Christmas is coming! Lucy and Tom are helping
to stir the Christmas pudding. As they stir they
each make a wish.

The postman comes to the house more often than usual. He brings cards wishing them all a merry Christmas, and sometimes packages too. These have to be hidden away until Christmas Day comes.

Lucy and Tom are making their own Christmas
cards with pictures of robins and Christmas trees
on them.

They've made some paper chains too, to
make the house look pretty. Mom is
putting up some green leaves.

On the hall table they've put a crib with Mary
and Joseph and Baby Jesus, the three kings, the
shepherds, and a donkey and a cow. Lucy and
Tom have cut out a big gold paper star to hang over
them and put pretend cotton-wool snow all
around.

They have presents for everybody in the family. Lucy has:

A sparkly pin for Mom.

An eraser in the shape of a dog for Dad to take to his office.

A comb in a case for Granny with A for Alison on it (because that's Granny's name).

A handkerchief for Grandpa with J for John on it (because that's Grandpa's name).

And a shiny blue car for Tom.

Tom has:

A mug for Mom to have her tea out of.

A smart bow-tie on an elastic for Dad.

A calendar for Granny which he made at nursery school.

A packet of seeds for Grandpa to grow flowers from when the spring comes.

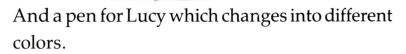

And a pen for Lucy which changes into different colors.

Lucy and Tom have wrapped up their presents already. Tom hides his in a different place every day. And every day he asks Lucy to guess what her present is going to be.

They talk a lot about the presents they hope they're going to get for Christmas.

Mom helps them both to write letters to Santa Claus and post them up the chimney.

There's a knock at the door. Some big children have come to sing carols.

One afternoon a band comes to their street to
play Christmas music. Lucy and Tom run out to
watch. They know some of the tunes. They can
sing *Silent Night*, *Away in a Manger* and *Once in
Royal David's City*.

Lucy and Tom go to the market with Dad to
choose a Christmas tree. There are crowds of
people. The lights are shining out and the shops
and stalls are full of exciting things.

Christmas Eve has come at last. Dad gets home early, and together they hang all sorts of pretty glittering things on the tree. Then they arrange the presents underneath it.

Now it's bedtime. Lucy and Tom hang up their
stockings at the end of their beds. They look out at the sky.
It's beginning to snow.

Mom says, "Good, it's going to be a white Christmas."

Lucy and Tom are *far* too excited to go to sleep. How can
you get to sleep when Santa Claus may be coming?

But somehow or other they do. When they wake up it's very early and still dark. It's Christmas Day. Has Santa Claus come? Yes, he has! Lucy and Tom feel into their stockings and pull out the presents one by one.

Lucy and Tom go along to Mom and Dad's room to show them what Santa Claus has brought. But it's a bit too soon for them yet. Imagine not wanting to wake up early on Christmas Day! Lucy and Tom go back to their room and play with their new toys.

Now Mom and Dad have woken up. They all hug each other. Christmas has really begun.

After breakfast they look out. It's white
everywhere and very cold. But the sun comes
out as they walk to church.

When they are at home again lots of people
arrive – Granny and Grandpa, Granny's old
friend Mrs Barlow who lives all by herself,
Aunty Jill and Uncle Rob and their little baby,
Elizabeth. That's ten people for dinner.
Everyone helps to get it ready.

They all sit down round the table to eat roast turkey, Christmas pudding and lots of other delicious things. Afterwards they pull crackers. There are some loud bangs, but Mrs Barlow doesn't mind a bit. She says she doesn't hear as well as she used to, and she just smiles and smiles.

After everything is cleared away, Lucy and
Tom give out a present for everyone from
underneath the tree. What a lot of surprises!

Elizabeth only likes the wrapping paper on
her present. She goes off to sleep in the middle
of it like a hamster.

Christmas can be quite tiring. Tom gets very
excited about his presents and rather cross.

So he and Grandpa go for a walk together in
the snow, just the two of them. The sun is very
big and red.

When they get home again, all the family sit round the fire and play Heads Bodies and Legs. The first person draws a head and folds over the paper, the next person draws a body, the next person draws some legs and the last person chooses a name. When they're all finished and the papers are opened out, there are some very funny looking pictures. Lucy calls her person "Uncle Rob" and Tom calls his "Santa Claus".

Now it's time to light the tree.

On earth peace, good will toward men.

It's dark outside. The lights shine out into the street. Merry Christmas, Lucy and Tom! Merry Christmas, everyone!